PUFFIN BOOKS
UK | USA | Canada | Ireland | Australia
India | New Zealand | South Africa

Puffin Books is part of the Penguin Random House group of companies
whose addresses can be found at global.penguinrandomhouse.com.

www.penguin.co.uk   www.puffin.co.uk   www.ladybird.co.uk

Penguin
Random House
UK

First published in Great Britain 2018
001
Copyright © Frederick Warne & Co. Ltd, 2018
Peter Rabbit™ & Beatrix Potter™ Frederick Warne & Co.
Frederick Warne & Co. is the owner of all rights, copyrights and
trademarks in the Beatrix Potter character names and illustrations

Printed in China
A CIP catalogue record for this book is available from the British Library

ISBN: 978–0–241–30176–0

All correspondence to:
Puffin Books
Penguin Random House Children's
80 Strand, London WC2R 0RL

LOVE

from PETER RABBIT

LOVE
is our
ADVENTURE

in the WORLD so BIG and WIDE,

IT'S THE
WAY WE
snuggle
up

WHEN THE
SUN
begins
to hide.

LOVE
IS HOW YOU
make
me
laugh

WHEN THE
times get
tough,

IT'S ALL
the smiles
YOU GIVE ME,

I WILL
never have
ENOUGH.

LOVE
IS HOW
you hold my hand

WHEN
I FEEL
a little
lost,

IT'S A *warm and cosy* FEELING

WHEN OUTSIDE
THERE'S
SNOW
and
FROST.

LOVE
will

BRIGHTEN *every* *day*

AND
shine
THROUGH

EVERY

night.

WHEN
WE ARE
together,

EVERYTHING
just feels
RIGHT.

SO *finally,*
THERE IS
ONE *thing*

THAT I
WOULD
like
to do...

IT'S TO
GIVE MY
hugs and kisses

and to
SAY THAT...

I love

you!